Bare

A Novella

Letti Raye Greene

Bare

First Edition
Copyright © 2024 Letti Raye Greene

All rights reserved.

ISBN: 9798333613806
Imprint: Independently published

All rights reserved. No part of this publication may be reproduced, stored or transmitted in any form or by any means, electronic, mechanical, photocopying, recording, scanning, or otherwise without written permission from the publisher and Author. It is illegal to copy this book, post it to a website, or distribute it by any other means without permission.

This novel is entirely a work of fiction. The names, characters, and incidents portrayed in it are the work of the author's imagination. Any resemblance to actual persons, living or dead, events or localities is entirely coincidental.

Letti Raye Greene asserts the moral right to be identified as the author of this work.

Letti Raye Greene has no responsibility for the persistence or accuracy of URLs for external or third-party Internet Websites
referred to in this publication and does not guarantee that any content on such Websites is, or will remain, accurate or appropriate.

Cover Art assembled and purchased from Canva by:
Letti Raye Greene

Canva Artists used:
@DebyQuynh
@Crocus Paperi
@CPP Design

Cover Model:
Barbie Carr

Author Photography by:
Melinda Parker-Fish

Bare

Dedication

To the sisters who claimed me, and the ones I claimed for myself.
To my daughter.
To my mother.
To my grandmother.
To my Mother-in-law.
To my Sister-in-law.
To my beautiful Nieces.
To Joanna.
To Julia.

To all those who have looked in a mirror and hated who and what they saw.

To all those who have had their body betray them.

To the fighters, to the survivors, and for all those we have lost.

Keep going. Keep Fighting.

Bare

CONTENTS

	Trigger/Content Warnings	9
Chapter 1	Early Arrivals and a Cold Goodbye	13
Chapter 2	Flying Clipboards and Leaking at Prom	23
Chapter 3	Lacy Reflections and Cheap Training Bras	35
Chapter 4	Big Glam and First Regrets	43
Chapter 5	Notes on Cheap Paper and Shitty Tips	53
Chapter 6	Hospital Highs and Bullshit Malls	61
Chapter 7	Sacrileges Jokes and a Lesbian Wedding	73
Chapter 8	Recovery Eviction & a Family Meeting	83
Chapter 9	Manbun in Scrubs and a Bullshit Diagnosis	93
Chapter 10	Promise of Sushi & a Rained out Date	101
Chapter 11	Shoe Shopping and Bare Chested	113
	Acknowledgment	
	About the Author	

Bare

Content-Trigger Warning

Before you begin, I wanted to list out the potential triggers in this Novella. It was very important for me as an author, but also as an avid reader to include Content/Trigger warnings for anyone who needs them. While I don't want anyone feeling the plot was ruined, I also want to respect your pain and your healing journey.

Most of these are just referenced and not graphically spelled out, but if you find you can't manage this, it is OK. I see you. You are valid, and so is your healing journey.

- **Foul language/Profanity**
- **Anxiety Attack**
- **Bigotry/Homophobia/Lesbiphobia**
- **Medical Treatments/Procedures**
- **Hospitalization**
- **Surgery**
- **Body Dysmorphia**
- **Bodily Fluids**
- **Bullying**
- **Emotional Abuse**
- **Gaslighting**
- **Child Abuse**
- **Drug Abuse**
- **Body Shaming**
- **Depression**
- **Cancer**
- **Religion/Purity Culture**
- **Death/Dying**

Bare

"Courage is a mean with regard to fear and confidence."

Aristotle

Bare

Chapter 1

Early Arrival and a Cold Goodbye

The sun wasn't even up yet, and the roads had been eerily quiet on the short drive in. The commute had been blissfully clear of any inept drivers or early morning deliveries. Just empty roads, dark skies, and her quiet Swedish electronica music. It was supposed to calm her and help her find some kind of center, at least that is what her therapist had told her. Her therapist had lied.

Gertrude had likely over packed and eyeing the backseat full of her homely comforts she felt embarrassed all over again. What kind of grown woman walks into a hospital for major surgery with a blankie and her favorite pillow? Apparently this one.

The car idled quietly as she rubbed her eyes under her four-year-old scratched glasses. She didn't normally wear them but all her pre-op papers told her not to wear her contacts, and Gertrude didn't feel like putting them in only to take them out a few hours later. It was the same with her piercings, She took them out and left them behind in the little brass bowl by her bed. Her burly, sloppy bulldog Albert licked her fingers with his tongue that was four times longer than it needed to be and never fit in his mouth. Gertrude missed her pup already.

The air conditioner was blowing cold, in the even colder morning. The crisp air kept her alert as she scanned up the high-rising hospital just beyond the parking garage she sat in. The side speckled with lights as some rooms were on, even at this ungodly hour. But most were off as the patient inside slept.

Gertrude's eyes grazed up the building counting the floors one by one. One, Two, Three, Four, and then stopping on Five. Hospice. Gertrude wrestled with the acute pain suddenly burrowing into the back of her skull as she turned the engine off and the world went dark except for the starlight of windows speckling the hospital. Unable to shake the darkness toying with her thoughts.

In the twilight and melancholy silence of her vehicle, Gertrude gave in and recalled the last time she had been there in that parking garage. The last time she had been there on floor five.

Up to that point, all of her treatments and care had been outpatient at the clinic just up the road from her condo. She had grown to love the people in office, while simultaneously hating the building, but she felt that it was justifiable. She had wanted to avoid the hospital at all costs, and they had helped her achieve that level of care. Until she couldn't any longer. Until treatments stopped working. She may have disliked the clinic. Here however Gertrude hated an entire floor and found nothing redeeming or lovable about it.

* * *

The hall smelled like death and lemons. It was quiet save for the soft music coming from the little chapel a few doors down and the respectful whispering from the nurses' station down the dim hall.

The threshold loomed in front of her, a harbinger of the past and pain. Things she had fought to move past and in that moment failed in doing so completely. The small rectangular window had a soft dim light inside, no sounds came from the the other side. The room of a dying woman. The room held so many questions and even more tears. Gertrude thought about turning around, taking her hand off the cold metal handle and walking away. No one would blame her; But time was up, and she saw movement behind that little pane of glass and she had to choose. Gertrude reached up to knock on the door when a small and glum figure jerked it open, her hand letting the handle slip away.

He was much shorter than she remembered, balding on top, and wore a scraggly brown shirt with tiny threadbare pin holes in it. He didn't particularly smell nice, like stale cigarettes, coffee, and unwashed hair. He was hunched over in what appeared to be a permanent slump, a cane grasped in his frail looking hands keeping him sort of upright. He looked tired and worn; Like it should be him hooked to those machines in there.

He looked up at her startled, but only for a moment. Then his face somehow went stoney despite the soft wrinkles. The iron he mined returned to his eyes in a way that reminded her of when she was a child, and he had been drinking. He tried to straighten up more, to meet her gaze dead on. He didn't manage. Gertrude had never been particularly tall but to see her father suddenly smaller than her was gut-wrenching and also kind of satisfying. This man of the house, this man's man, had become a small dirty mouse of a creature that came up to her chin.

He eyed her cautiously, years of unspoken vitriol bubbling up under the surface of both of them and Gertrude decided to end it before it got started. She nodded her head, acknowledging him and then she sidestepped around him and entered the room. Her father also made the mature choice and let Gertrude pass, shutting the door behind him and disappearing down the hall. Maybe they were both too tired to fight. Gertrude let out her breath, louder than she meant to, and the form lying in the bed moved with strained and slow movements.

The room was warm, not cold like the rest of the hospital. A few vases in the corner of the room stood out with their decay and paper-thin flowers. A small breeze would have torn them apart. A few cards on the table next to the bed, they looked hand drawn and childish, probably from Walter's Sunday school class he taught. The old little radio clock had been removed from its place in Gertrude's childhood home and sat out of place on the table. A stagnant glass of water, and the worn bible she had always carried.

Beady blue eyes, clouded by strong medication and age had locked onto her, and

Gertrude suddenly became ten years old again. Her mother became the towering force of nature that had beaten against Gertrude until they both broke and then they did it again. Gertrude approached the bed and sat in the vacant chair, her mother's eyes still on her, still playing predator versus prey even on her deathbed.

The bed had an old quilt on it, one Gertrude's grandmother had made, a comfort from home. Gertrude's tried to find words, or even emotions to relay, something other than the fear and shame she had felt at that moment. She wanted to tell her about everything going on, about Oliver and the baby. About Claire and the high-profile clients she booked. About her, and what she was going through. Gertrude tugged at her long black sleeves hiding her arms and her head tightly but consciously covered with an elaborate wrap Clair had gotten for her. Gertrude became keenly aware of her own sunken features; her sallow skin. The bones in her own thin fingers as she reached out to grasp her mother's hand, seeing a reflection in her she needed.

Her mother groaned and rolled away, refusing to look at Gertrude anymore. Gertrude's voice was small then, returned to that little girl who wanted to be comforted, to be coddled like a child that small should be, "Mommy, please." It was all she could muster. The sob lodged in her throat.

Her mother's raspy voice returned, still cold and distant, but a ghost of the booming and strong resonance it had once been, "Let me die in peace."

Gertrude stayed a little while longer. She wasn't sure if it was spite or some unfulfilled need she had to try and find love where there wasn't any. She wanted to say something, and for her mother to say a lot of things. But even in the end, neither of them could or would.

As Gertrude left the room, closing the door softly behind her, her father approached from the side. He didn't meet her gaze as he simply said, "It's best if you do not come to the funeral. Joy will call you when it's done." Then without any comfort or affection, he disappeared behind the door to be with his wife.

Gertrude left the hospital, and her parents behind. She never told Oliver she went.

****

Gertrude hit the button on the elevator too many times. Her rolling glittery black suitcase behind her, her favorite blanket and pillow tucked securely under her arm. The stuffed dinosaur was hidden in the suitcase, a photo of her, Claire, and Albert rolled up safely in her pajamas. She didn't care if anyone judged her, fuck them, she was having major surgery.

Stepping into the vacant lift she eyed the button with the big black number five on it. Gertrude wondered if maybe her mother's ghost roamed the halls of floor five haunting the nurses and torturing the dying. Maybe Gertrude should visit. Maybe she would join her soon enough.

Gertrude shook away the tendrils of the past and darkness eating up her spine and hit the number eight. With a start, the elevator jumped and then moved on. Gertrude needed to as well.

Bare

Chapter 2

Flying Clipboards & Leaking in the Bathroom

Gertrude sat with the cheap plastic clipboard awkwardly balanced on her knee as she tried to fish out her insurance card and ID from her coffin wallet. Why all this information didn't carry over from the one office to the hospital, she didn't know. Especially since it had all been planned for weeks and they all shared the same computers. Gertrude slid the cards under the metal clip and flipped to the last two of the ten million pages that needed her attention. It hadn't really been that many, but Gertrude had signed less paperwork when they had bought the condo. Gertrude shook off her annoyance and looked at the white pages that needed her attention. It was emergency contact information, well that was easy enough, and then the dreaded DNR.

Gertrude had gone back and forth mentally on this topic for weeks. Since they finally settled down and agreed to do this. It felt all contradictory and almost like a bait and switch. All the doctors told her the same thing, it's a 'pretty standard surgery done a hundred times a day nothing to worry about' to an 'in the event you die situation'.

Gertrude knew things happened, but she wasn't even forty yet, and no other obvious health problems, was there really a chance she could die. If she did die and they brought her back what kind of shit would everyone else put her through.

What would her death put them through? Even then, she couldn't help feeling a bit played by the whole thing and lost at what to do.

The emotional overload this one piece of paper had put her through had been oppressive. And now here she was the moment of impending need and she was indecisive. If she did sign it, it would be a lot easier on everyone than the long recovery ahead. They could just bury her and mourn.

Maybe it was the thought of trying to find her mother and giving her a piece of her mind in the afterlife if there was one. Maybe it was Claire, and burdening her with the title of caregiver. Lone threads of self-doubt and that feeling of being a burden creepy crawled up Gertrude's skin in droves like spiders breaking loose of a web sack. Filling her insides with self-loathing, self-pity, and self-doubt.

Quickly and without a second thought she clenched her eyes shut and signed the DNR. It was lopsided and not all the way on the line, but good enough. Gertrude buried in the very back of the half-inch stack of forms she had filled out this morning not wanting to think about it or the after effects of that crooked signature.

She jumped up from the uncomfortable wood and cheap leather chair she had been stuck to and bolted for the desk to drop off the paperwork. Her own two overly eager feet tripped over each other as gracelessly as a drunken Dodo, and she slammed into the large desk shoulder first. The clipboard flew out of her hands and landed on the other side with a clattering sound.

The two women behind the desk snorted in amusement and then quickly tried to cover it up with feigned concern as they gathered up the papers that ha askew. They failed. The laughs kept catching in their throats. Gertrude wished they had choked on them.

A strained conversation with a few stifled laughs later, and Gertrude limped back to her chair rubbing her shoulder, flushed with fresh embarrassment and she desperately wished she had clocked one of them in the head with a wayward clipboard. The sound of the mocking giggles at her back followed her and echoed in her soul. Gertrude changed chairs and sat in one with her back to them. Like it was high school all over again.

* * *

They say Prom was a great right of passage, leaving behind your school days to face the world as an adult. For Gertrude, it felt like just another school dance. Too many people, too many hormones. She had come with some friends, but they had partnered off to slow dance and get a few sloppy kisses and ill-disguised gropes in. Gertrude kept the shawl she swiped from her mother around her shoulders and clasped it tightly across her torso with a hand. She had let a friend talk her into the worst idea imaginable and Gertrude knew she was going to regret it, so instead she prudishly tired to hide it.

The chaperones did not give a single fuck that night, since the next time they would see all the seniors again would be when they were in cap and gowns, why not let them run roughshod, it was after all prom. Gertrude was almost certain that Principal Mason was sipping from a flask that was poorly hidden in the blazer jacket that went out of style two decades ago and was at least two sizes too small. He was overly friendly and handsy with the students and the female staff. And he reeked. It was nauseating to be near him.

Gertrude sauntered up slowly to the picked-over buffet of cheap snacks, soggy sandwiches, and lukewarm punch. The crumbs littered the floor under her as her hand-me-down wedges were accidentally ground into powder and grit under her. Gertrude snatched up one of the little finger eclairs with her free hand and popped it in her mouth, the inside still cold from when they had been frozen a few hours prior. Nothing else on the table looked particularly appetizing and Gertrude abandoned it altogether.

The lights pulsed in time with the slow melodic rhythm of a recently released sappy love song as it belted out over the speakers and washed over the dance floor. Units of two peppered the wide space, most staring adoringly at each other. Some in that awkward arms-length distance dance swaying side to side out of rhythm, and others practically under one another's skin grinding together with very good rhythm. Gertrude had to get away from both. Her sloppy attempt to escape the dance area was thwarted by a boy whose name she didn't remember, a hopeful look in his eyes and a mustard stain on his rented tuxedo shirt. No way was she going to dance with him. She had to get out of there.

Escaping the boy and the dancing couples, Gertrude practically ran down a hall and to the girl's bathroom. Only when she stepped inside she nearly stumbled right back out again. The skunky smell of illicit substances was like a brick wall she hadn't expected to run into in the Band Hallway. Peering through the clam-baked haze she saw a few girls she didn't know but two girls she was very familiar with, and decided it was best to turn around and go back.

They, however, had other plans.

"Gertie! Stay. You wanna hit?" She hated being called Gertie.

Gertrude shook her head and turned to leave when hands seized her shoulders and dragged her deeper into the mist of the bathroom. Gertrude couldn't remember her name, maybe it was Sam, she wasn't sure, but she remembered everything else about her clearly. Round face, with a brown pixie cut. She had blue eyes and a sing-song voice that always sounded like it was mocking you.

She was a high-functioning stoner, and a pretty good basketball player apparently. She won some trophies last year and the whole team won a huge one this year. They even did an assembly to celebrate them, in which afterward Gertrude ran into them smoking. Guess you still need to get high even when you are on top of the world. Rumors swirled she had already landed some scholarship for college to play basketball. She wasn't a senior, but she had dated enough of them that it shouldn't have been surprising she was here at prom.

Gertrude had bought from her a few times, but when it didn't in fact fix Gertrude's life she stopped buying and moved on to some other bad habits that were just as fleeting as the first. A fact that the girl had been a bit bitter about as she overcharged Gertrude and liked to brag about it. When the blunt was offered to her Gertrude shook her head again, "No thanks. I didn't mean to interrupt your party." Her hands clenched the strained fabric around her torso tighter.

Unfazed, the stoner girl whose likely name was Sam, took another hit and then flicked the joint at Gertrude. Sparks landed on the delicate but cheap fabric wrapped around her as it burned and curled into hard bits of melted something. Gertrude flailed erratically in an attempt not to get burned, her hands released all the tension and her humiliation was on full display as Gertrude stamped the burning shawl, the girl laughed.

"Did you get a boob job? Look at that padding!" All eyes turned to Gertrude and she froze. Another in the bathroom, someone Gertrude couldn't see clearly spoke up, "Nah! It's one of them water bras." Then the previously jovial bathroom became menacingly silent, and all that was heard was, "Pop it!"

Hands seized Gertrude's shoulders, and her mother's shawl lay ruined on the filthy floor. Gertrude didn't cry out, or really struggle even. She went stone-faced, something she had learned from her father. From nowhere, a safety pin was produced and the damage was done. As the warm oily liquid seeped down the front of her, staining the satin dress, she kept her eyes locked on the paper towel dispenser. Ignoring their laughs and observations of the liquid.

Even when the bullies and stoners cleared out leaving her there she memorized every dent in the metal, the shape of the keyhole, the way the jagged edge of the paper towel looked like the border of a continent on some foreign map. The music eventually quieted and in the end, Gertrude did not leave that bathroom until the entire school had emptied.

She left the shawl on the floor and had her diploma mailed to her.

**

Gertrude tried to flip through the paperback book she had brought, but the snickering behind the desk was wearing her down. She slammed it shut louder than she had intended and shoved it back into her bag. She wished she had a joint right then. Not the shitty stuff from high school but something good and mellow, but she wasn't feeling sick, and thus wouldn't have been able to justify it. And given she was in a hospital, phoning a friend for a gummy would have been frowned upon. Besides she would be out and in the blackness of surgery soon enough, she just had to survive this.

Gertrude fished back out her book and tried to turn back to her misplaced page, but couldn't find it. And if she was honest she had immediately forgotten what was written on the previous one she had read. The hushed chortles quieted down suddenly in the presence of a third nurse behind the counter. A hushed but disapproving voice came from that direction, chastising the ladies. Gertrude refused to look. She hoped they were getting reprimanded like children, but she decided wouldn't gloat about it. At least not in front of them.

Gertrude continued to blindly flip through the pages of her book a moment longer before finally giving it up again. She returned her book to the bag and shifted her weight in the chair, eager to escape it to her hospital room and hide from the eyes of any passersby.

The clock ticked slowly. Too slow. Gertrude was going to fish the book out again for the third time, however she was saved by a familiar tutting. Nurse Schultz from the clinic tapped on the table next to Gertrude.

"Come on lazy bones, let's get you to your room. It's your big day."

Chapter 3

Lacy Reflections and Cheap Training Bras

Gertrude stood there tilting her head this way and that way, admiring them in the mirror for the last time. The whir of the machines angrily sounded just beyond the stark and sterile bathroom, yelling for her to come back and appropriately reattach them. She ignored them and would continue until the nurse came in to yell at her. Which, if Nurse Schultz stayed true to character, it would be any minute.

Gertrude turned to the side again and admired the silhouette of her torso. She smiled and ran her fingers over her breasts. They were never more than a small palm full at best, something she both loved and had hated at various points in her life. The small upturn of flesh looked cute under the harsh light of the fluorescent bulbs, despite everything else. Her nipples still carried the small scars of piercings that had been removed and healed. Her skin was covered in little goose pimples.

The small and absolutely undeserved stretch marks lead up into her armpit and collarbone like scars of lightning along her skin. The tattoo of stars smattering over her chest and dipped down her sternum, between the small mounds of flesh, stretched and moved slightly with her shallow breaths. Gertrude had never really looked at herself before, but she wasn't ugly, despite the abnormally small boobs.

The bra hanging off the peg on the door, a black lacy number she had worn to feel sexy, was a reminder of what she had and what she didn't. "Sexy at a hospital is a cry for help." Claire had said to her that morning as she slathered the newest and darkest lip gloss she could on her lips. Gertrude rolled her eyes at Claire and pulled on the matching lacey underwear for added effect, knowing full well Claire would still stare at her. Go big or go home they say and when Gertrude flirted she went big. Gertrude's boobs must have heard that saying however and ran for home as fast as they could, cause big was not something they understood.

Somehow that morning seemed like a year ago and the black bra hanging off that hook was no longer sexy. Just a cruel reminder. Gertrude, despite herself, remembered with a melancholic smile her first bra was nothing like the black lacy number taunting her on the door. It was painful, and life-altering.

✶ ✶ ✶

Gertrude was eleven years old, flushed hot with embarrassment and utter humiliation as her mother unceremoniously held up plain, or just plain ugly, training bras. Her mother was loudly tutting at the shape of the garments or fabric they came in, the printed patterns on them or the color of the bra. The store was bustling and a few roaming eyes fell on Gertrude as carts passed by, from jealous younger girls to creepy old men, they all had eyes for her and immediately went to gawk at Gertrude's torso.

Her protests fell on deaf ears and were met with hard slaps at her hands as she tried to push away the industrial strength flattener her mother wanted her to wear. A couple of girls a few years older could be seen snickering at her from a few racks over, indiscreetly hiding their glee over her embarrassment as they pretended to look through shirts they clearly had no interest in. One even took to mimicking Gertrude's mother as she sneered at the price.

Gertrude remembers crossing her arms over the buds of adolescence barely growing at her chest. Hot tears, and the need for therapy that she would procrastinate on getting, building up under her rib cage. She tried to turn it off then, that was the first time for that too, shutting down. Closing it all off and living as an empty shell. There but not really there, just hollow. Gertrude was never quite sure how she did it. Apparently, it's a trauma response to which, when told, Gertrude looked at her therapist and very sarcastically shrugged with a, "You think doc?" That was the end of that session and a script for a new dosage of her meds.

Her mom bought that white, too-tight sports bra that kept her flat-chested for just a little while longer.

The car ride home was full of her mother talking about sin and periods and sin again. Reminding her that she was cursed with Eve's curse and her nakedness was shameful. New rules were in place with immediate effect. With the appearance of her very small boobs her whole life had changed overnight.

Gertrude's dad began yelling at her about wearing tank tops around without the "girdle" on. She wasn't allowed to curl up on his lap anymore and he wouldn't tuck her in anymore. He went from doting on her to ignoring her.

Suddenly she had to wear a T-shirt over her bathing suit, even around her brothers and she wasn't allowed to sleep in their room anymore. They weren't allowed in hers. She was lectured on the place of a woman, how to behave, and how to dress. Her shirts were two sizes too big, and she was lectured about wearing anything that went above her knee.

Her pastor sat her and two other girls down, girls whose names Gertrude couldn't recall, and gave them chastity rings and preached to them about saving themselves for marriage. Saving what? Why was it just them there? Where were the boys? Some of her first questions about puberty reverberated well into her twenties. And shame and embarrassment followed suit. These stupid tiny little things ruined her life and robbed her of her childhood.

***

"Gertie, you need to be in bed. The doctor is coming in to go over all the pre-op stuff with you." The knocks rattled the bathroom door and shook the memories free. Gertrude hated being called Gertie.

She sighed and flushed the toilet for a misleading alibi. "One second." She returned with a strained cheerfulness in her voice. Gertrude pulled up her hospital gown and retied the ties at her sides. The gaudy fabric overwhelmed her frame and hid the breasts she had grown to hate, then love, then hate again. At the present they, her breasts, and her were not seeing eye to eye. It was a typical toxic love-hate relationship.

She washed her hands quickly, foregoing soap as she hadn't actually used the toilet. Splashing some water on her face she wiped away the tears and the past and took a deep breath to steady herself. She couldn't look back at that anymore.

She opened the door to Nurse Schultz's kind but disapproving look hovered at eye level. "Come on Gertie honey let's get you back into bed and ready. It's a big day!" Gertrude looked in

Bare

the mirror one last time and then followed Nurse Schultz out shutting the light off in the bathroom. Leaving the reflection and who she was behind. She really hated being called Gertie.

Chapter 4

Big Glam Make-up and First Regrets

Settling into the uncomfortable bed with the itchy sheets Gertrude grimaced as the thermometer was shoved a little too aggressively under her tongue. Nurse Schultz was kind of a hard ass but a sweet hard ass if that made sense. The blood pressure cuff beeped as it released Gertrude's arm from the death grip. Tip tapping away the information into the computer next to the bed, Nurse Schultz tutted her disapproval of the numbers on the screen. So Gertrude's blood pressure was a bit high, she didn't know what they expected of her.

Gertrude sighed and laid back as Nurse Schultz bustled around. She felt that little switch inside trying to flip. To turn off and go numb. It would be easy, and maybe make all this easier. Quick and painless she could just ease through this whole ordeal. Gertrude had wanted to so many times through this process, but something or someone stopped her. She closed her eyes and felt the clicking of the metaphoric tumblers in her locked box of poor coping mechanisms when a shuffle of feet and the tsking from the Nurse pulled her away from the black box of self-induced pestilence and back into the hospital room she would be residing in for the foreseeable future.

Gertrude opened an eye and smiled, unsurprised and somewhere deep inside relieved at the brightest soul she knew lighting up the room. "Hey, Nurse Sarah! You looking good today girl! When you ganna leave that husband of yours and come to the dark side? We have cookies!" Claire couldn't help but flirt. She didn't mean much by it, but she was exceptional at it.

Nurse Schultz rolled her big brown eyes at Claire, refusing to answer her, and turned to Gertrude. "The Doctor will be in soon. You rest." She left quickly, probably to get away from Claire who noisily dragged a chair over to the bed. Her composure still holding strong as she took Gertrude's hand and kissed her forehead. She settled in and Gertrude saw the forced smile she was putting on and deep inside she went reaching for the lockbox again.

Gertrude smiled and squeezed her hand. "How was the Bridal party?" Talking about work always perked Claire up. Even if she acted like she hated it, she loved her job and it was way better than where she used to work.

"Atrocious. The bride gave me some pop star princess photos for inspiration and wanted to go big glam. Which I am on board with. You know me, I love doing big glam. The bigger the glammier the better. Then her mother walked in and lost her shit. So we had to clean her face and start fresh with a mommy-approved look." Gertrude chuckled as Claire continued, "Then there was a hubbub about the dress, apparently the father of the bride thought there were sleeves on the strapless dress. All causing a crisis of morals and a bunch of quiet laughter from me as I packed up as fast as I could. All her mom kept shrieking was 'YOUR BOOBS ARE ON DISPLAY!'"

They both stopped suddenly, Claire's face falling and she squeezed Gertrude's hand, an apology prepared to pour out from her black glossed lips. But they were saved by the ill-timed knock and entrance of the surgeon who would lead her surgery today. He glanced at them, and then down to his paperwork. He came back up to focus on their clasped hands and then resumed. He smiled, that smile Gertrude had come to expect from men who didn't quite expect two women to be married or how to handle it. But he was good at pushing it aside and stepping up to the proverbial plate and taking charge, as Gertrude expected, he felt expected to do.

Gertrude gripped harder at Claire's hand, and she squeezed back. Time to get this parade moving, and the rest of the surgical team entered with smiles and blue scrubs on. They looked as hopeful as Gertrude felt hollow.

The conversation seemed to pass mostly in a blur. Claire asked a lot of questions about the recovery, what she needed to do, and how to help. The doctor, his name escaped Gertrude no matter how hard she tried to hold on to it, kept his bedside manner clipped but professional. The back and forth over her went on for a bit until suddenly the room was too quiet.

Gertrude looked around and saw that a number of the staff had left and the main surgeon and Claire were both waiting for her response, "Sorry, I was distracted." He nodded empathetically and repeated in a soft baritone, "Can you lower the gown so we can do a quick examination."

Gertrude nodded and sat up and loosed the ties at the side of her gown. At some point, Nurse Schultz had returned and stood quietly in the corner, a reassuring and protective nature to her as she watched the Doctor, more than Gertrude. The doctor washed his hands and with the same soft baritone asked Claire to step outside. Gertrude squeezed her hand and she didn't move. Choking on the words a bit Gertrude spoke up, "No, she stays." He stopped and looked at her, a series of unidentifiable but easily guessed, emotions played over his face but he just nodded. That professionalism getting the better of him again.

His gloved hands moved around her torso in a deliberate and thankfully clinical manner, feeling and pressing in the most uncomfortable and borderline painful ways. It reminded Gertrude of her very clumsy first time with an equally clumsy boy.

* * *

They were hiding in his parent's basement under the guise of studying. It was dim with a crappy lone incandescent lightbulb lighting their clumsy endeavor. The air reeked of his dad's smuggled cigarettes and mold. Her only other company was the long worn cobwebs vacant of any eight-legged terrors. His name was Joe, and he too moved his hands over her body in a semi-clinical manner. More like she was a figurine fresh from the package and less like she was the girl he had made out with at the park two hours ago.

Up to that point they had only just made out, but at seventeen, Gertrude was desperate to belong somewhere. Drugs and grades, good and bad of both, had failed her multiple times. So sex seemed like the logical next step for an incredibly illogical teenager. Hormones had caught up, or desperation, or both.

Joe's hands cupped her breast easily, really nothing for him to hold on to, as his fingers grazed at her collarbone. The whole of her fit into his palm with ease. His brow had furrowed and seemed disappointed when he ineptly pulled off her shirt and bra to examine her closer. Gertrude had always wondered what he had been thinking in that moment, but then sanity prevailed and she always decided it was best if she didn't know.

Gertrude remembers thinking to herself, "Yeah I am disappointed too." His tongue scraped across her nipple leaving a slimy trail that disgusted Gertrude. She should have known then that he, and really his whole sex, wouldn't be what she wanted in life. However religious trauma dies slowly, and as he thrust into her she stared at the chastity ring on her finger. Her hands were on his shoulders and her body moved numbly in time with him. She didn't look at him, and the pain went away with a quick turn of her internal key. She went through the motions, not really sure if she was supposed to like it. She didn't. He would later, when they inevitably did it again and then again, brag about her transition to womanhood as he would finish into the stinky little glow-in-the-dark condoms. His claim to her virginity was something that helped him get off.

Afterward, she lay on the musty blanket sprawled out on the cold tiled basement floor, his lanky fingers still stroking her small breast in what one would almost think was loving. The smell of him, his spit and his seed had long since turned her stomach sour and she kept her neck stiff and her head staring off into the darkness of the basement. Gertrude wouldn't look at him. He asked her nonchalantly, "You ever think about getting a boob job?" Gertrude never talked to him again.

She went home later that night and locked her screaming mother outside the bathroom as she showered in water so hot it nearly blistered her skin. Gertrude didn't remember crying, just sitting there numb, but she liked to think she did.

***

"Ok, Gertie you are good. All set to sit up." Gertrude sat back up quickly, her arms instinctually came up to cover her chest, letting the nickname slide despite Nurse Schultz's wicked smile. The doctor pulled the computer up and started typing in some notes, his gloves discarded to the side and not even in the trash. Then with no other feigned pleasantries, he mumbled some instructions to Nurse Schultz and left the room. Just another "Feel and Flee" as Gertrude liked to call them. What was it about lesbian breasts that made male doctors turn absolute idiot?

Claire helped Gertrude tie the hospital gown back up and get re-situated in the bed as comfortably as she could. Nurse Schultz cleared away the mess the inconsiderate doctor had left the annoyance plain on her face. Gertrude thought good, she deserved it for the "Gertie" joke.

She gave them a small smile and then left the room with the promise of a sedative to help calm Gertrude's nerves before they started the pre-op routine.

Almost time.

Chapter 5

Notes on Cheap Paper and Shitty Tips

Claire managed to look more afraid than Gertrude felt. But it had been like that since they started this entire horse and pony show. Gertrude pulled Claire closer and kissed her. The room was finally empty, save for them, and she was in the mood to take all her lasts as she could get them.

Claire's lips were velvety, the matte lip gloss smelled of fruit and musk, with a hint of the mint toothpaste they had at home. Gertrude kissed her again, nothing desperate or sexy. Nothing to write a novel about, just loving, sweet even. So many unspoken words failed to take shape even as their two mouths pressed together. But even when they said nothing, they said everything they could.

Gertrude felt a lump well up in her throat as Claire lingered at her lips before letting out a sad little sigh and sitting down in the chair again. Silently she pulled out a black little notebook, usually reserved for her clients, their pallets, skin types, and any allergies they had. When Claire did her make-up consults she took down a lot of information, even swatches and preferred brands. She was very organized and repeat clients like her models had their own files and portfolios back at the condo.

Claire turned to a whole new page, pulled the pen from the spiral, and started jotting down her notes from the doctor's visit. Soft scratching on the paper as Gertrude turned to stare at the fluorescent lights in the speckled recessed ceiling felt hypnotic almost. The next few months of her life whittled down to graphite on pressed and dried wood pulp. She wouldn't be a person but a sheet of recovery instructions.

The quiet hum the lights gave off grew louder as Gertrude focused on hearing it. Tuning out the pen, the damned paper, and the fucking machines connected to her. Gertrude wanted to drown out the sounds of wound care and infection signs. The steps needed to ensure her mental health stayed positive, and her bandage changes were done correctly. The talks of physical therapy after and possible reconstruction.

Gertrude felt reduced to a cheap pencil on dollar store paper. Something small, so tawdry, and seemingly out of Gertrude's current emotional range.

The humming from the lights was the same humming she had heard when she worked at a diner, once upon a time.

Bare

* * *

The maintenance guy stepped down off the old metal ladder still blocking Gertrude from getting to the much needed coffee pot. She could hear the angry whispers from her tables as she failed to bring them their bean brewed elixir of life. Not that she'd drink any of it, with its burnt aftertaste and bitter swill, it left all the cups with a layer of silt at the bottom. She just had to grab the pot and take it to tables three, four, and five, but it was out of reach. And the longer this man kept his ladder in her way, her tips dwindled down cent by cent.

Finally, with a grunt and a loud scraping clatter, the ladder was out of her way, and with a metaphorical fire under her ass she tried to deliver out the coffees, waters, and greasy foods to the select clientele that frequented a 24-hour diner at 2 am.

Not a one of them looked clean, and Gertrude was sure not a one of them was sober. Some she was sure came in with a variety of spirits in their systems, and bodily fluids on their clothes. One time a girl came in with a dribble of vomit still rolling down her chin. But they came anyway, in waves like clock work. One would leave, with a messy table, half empty plates, and a shitty tip and the next would file in eager to fill the vacated seat.

Gertrude pushed through it night after night, her fake smile and sluggish demeanor clashed and left some of her tables feeling off. Just like outside of work, her personality was too broken for solid connections.

Around four in the morning, just as the bar rush ended, the early birds started making their way in. Usually police and other responders. They usually didn't say much to her, but tonight was special. The other waitress had called off, and what should have been a stellar opportunity to rake in more tips ended up in Gertrude quitting her job.

He was in construction, or at least he looked it. His table of mid twenties young guys made him look like a grandpappy surrounded by his grandkids. He certainly talked over them and for them like he was their patriarch. Ordering them each a black coffee and a cheese omelet. He didn't however foot the bill. He barked at them when they refused to speak up and slammed his hand down, causing all the dishes to chime.

One poor boy at the table it mousy eyes and hair had truly earned his ire. The old man had been barking about his wife. Gertrude was refilling the coffees when he boomed out, "Peter you got a woman yet?" Gangly and mousy Peter, with his curls and still full coffee, stutter fell short. "Speak up boy? You got a woman?" Peter didn't respond after that, he just lowered his eyes to the cup in front of him. Then the old man noticed Gertrude, and said "I'd tell you to ask this one out, make her a wife and a mother, but she ain't got no titties." In a well rounded mix of amusement and horror, the table of boys in their thick cargo pants and fluorescent vests met Gertrude's gaze.

She was frozen, however, locked in a staring contest she didn't agree to participate in, and unsure of who is winning. Her cheeks flushed with heat that she felt creep into her hairline. It was when grandpappy pulled her shirt out a bit she came too and smacked the crap out of him.

The table sounded with hoots of laughter as the loud man was finally silenced. Gertrude turned silently, with one hand grabbing her last shitty tip off the next table, and left the diner.

She always hoped Peter found a better job.

*** * * ***

The scratching had stopped and it had barely registered for Gertrude when the bed shifted next to her as Claire climbed in. Her smile was infectious as Gertrude returned it, opening her arms for Claire to snuggle in. She smelled of faint musky perfume and faintly of their dog Albert. They lay there for a time. Quite, still, and content. This was the happiest Gertrude had been in months. She could forget they were in a hospital and just at home. Or even on a vacation. Shame the setting wasn't Paris or Aruba.

Claire kissed Gertrude's cheek and pulled out her new phone with its already cracked screen. She held it up on selfie mode and Gertrude locked in on herself. "For posterity babe!" Claire had said and she quickly leaned in to fix her eyeliner and then pushed a curl from her face. Gertrude snatched up a beanie cap and slid it over her head. Gertrude then nodded and smiled. She leaned in, squeezing her face into the picture as she pushed the humming in her ears aside and smiled for the selfie. For posterity.

Claire took way too many selfies.

CHAPTER 6

Hospital Highs and Bullshit Malls

They had given Gertrude the good meds, her mind was light and her body was buzzing. Nurse Schultz had come in and taken all her blood work and put her IV in. She had given the bag a shot of something that kicked in almost right away. She hummed a happy tune and kept a reassuring smile on her face. When another, older nurse popped her head in, she stared at Gertrude and Claire for just a little too long before asking, "Sarah you need any help in here." Nurse Schultz quick to fire back, "This lovely couple doesn't need anything else but thoughts and prayers right now. Thanks, Jodie." Her voice lilted with sarcasm masked in sickly sweet.

Jodie scrunched up her face and closed the door in slow motion, still gawking at the couple until she almost pinched her overly chubby cheeks in the door. Nurse Schultz shook her head as she finished typing in whatever she had been working on. She looked over at an overly cheerful Gertrude and smiled, "We don't need any bigots in here bothering you before you go in do we, sweetie?" Gertrude giggled. She wasn't sure why, but she did but it felt right.

Claire stepped out to call her mom and update her. They were really close and talked a lot, not something Gertrude really understood, but at that moment she didn't care. Nurse Schultz went to follow her out the door, chastising Gertrude for asking if she could have a big ass burger, fries, and chocolate shake. To be fair she was prompted when Nurse Schultz asked if she needed anything else.

Nurse Schultz meant well and took all of Gertrude's poorly timed dark humor in stride. Saying as she closed the door, "No you are officially pre op, and I am a vegetarian so I wouldn't bring it to you anyways." Gertrude giggled again and shouted after her, "But you asked!" and then for some unknown reason laughed loudly and the door shut.

It was quiet again. Her body crawled with the high she was feeling, the sensation of caring but not caring about caring washed over her mind in waves of chemically induced bliss. She knew it was the medication, but somehow she couldn't care. It was a circle of incomplete thoughts and feelings.

The soft beep of her phone kept going off, likely someone on social media commenting on the photos Claire had shared. A show of hopeful positivity during this trying time Gertrude giggled again and said out loud, "It's bullshit." Just like the stupid day when the stupid doctor had given her the stupid news. Bullshit.

* * *

Malls were bullshit. Gertrude's friend, Betty had brought her along to shop for a backless bra. The wedding they were both in was just a few weeks away and Gertrude had slacked off on getting here due to the embarrassment likely to ensue. For someone with no boobs, getting a backless bra to support and smooth something she didn't have was a recipe for embarrassment. She muttered to Betty over and over again that it was bullshit. She hated the mall.

Gertrude had tried some local big-name shops, but it had proven to be useless and she had ended up here anyways. Betty perused the naughty wear, looking for something to seduce one of the groomsmen in, while Gertrude tried to look invisible and not draw the associate's attention to her. She just wanted to find one and get out. No measuring tapes, no conversation.

Gertrude remembered feeling guilty somehow like she was intruding on a space not meant for her or her tiny boobs. She turned and kept her head down skimming through the sports bras she didn't want or need. But Gertrude knew if she looked like she was lost, someone was going to approach her.

Gertrude tried to move through the racks with a feigned knowledge she didn't have. Trying to look without moving her head around, side-eye everything without giving it away she was hopeless. Unfortunately, she managed to garner the attention of an overly zealous girl, eager to make a sale and get the minuscule commission she must get from selling overpriced bras with practically nothing to them. Gertrude's plan had failed, and she started to hear this soft ringing in her ear and felt her fingertips tingle with a pins and needles sensation.

The girl's smile was bright and too white, the residue of this morning's whitening strip clung the the inner corner of her lips and the overly gelled and slicked back ponytail bobbed in time with the volume at her chest. Gertrude immediately wished she could disappear into the rack of negligees or even run from the store screaming. Instead, she shifted her weight, pulled the black denim jacket tighter around her, and crossed her arms over her chest.

The smile with boobs came up and the pink nametag revealed her name to be Sam, probably short for Samantha. She didn't look like Sam from high school, she was too sweet. Her perky demeanor would likely have been contagious to anyone else but made Gertrude clam up even more. Sam smiled wider, if that was possible, her fingers twiddling the measuring tape draped freely over her shoulders. "Can I help you feel beautiful today?" Her tone was nauseatingly pleasant and borderline genuine. Gertrude cleared her own throat and just shook her head with a quiet, "No, I just need to get a backless bra."

Taking the challenge up as if invited to, Sam's smile defied the laws of physics and grew wider. "Absolutely! Right this way." She turned and with one last futile glance at Betty begging her for help that never came, Gertrude followed silently. Still squeezing her ribcage tight trying to keep the pounding her her heart inside.

The backless bras were quite literally in the back corner of the store. It happened to also be the most crowded part, wedding and prom season in full swing everyone and their mother needed a specialty bra.

Sam turned back to Gertrude, and with a swift, nearly unseen, movement pulled the measuring tape from her neck and reached out to Gertrude to push her hands aside. It was all very reactionary, and Gertrude didn't even realize what she had done until it was over and the other customers, Sam and even Betty in the distance looked at her like she was nuts. It was then the words softly reverberated off the walls and back to her in an echo cutting through the store's poppy music, "Stop it. Don't touch me."

Gertrude hadn't remembered shouting it, but the small sharp pang in her throat confirmed she had. Her arms had shot out in front of her, not close enough to push Sam away but to keep her from coming closer. The measuring tape hung limp in her hand swaying side to side at the holder was perfectly still. Sam just started laughing, her once genuine smile turned sour and cruel. "Sweety you don't need a bra anyways, there's nothing there."

Gertrude turned away, the sensation of being weighed down pulled at her limbs as she fought with her body to get to the door. It was like trying to run through clavicle-deep mud. The edges of her vision started going dark and cloudy and the only thing she could hear was the gasping panicked sound of her own breathing being drowned out by a shrill mechanical scream coming from everywhere all at once. She reached out to grasp at a metal display to help stabilize her but she didn't quite make it. In the distance, Betty stared in a mix of horror and embarrassment before stepping out of the store, her intended purchases discarded on a shelf.

Gertrude tried to focus on one foot in front of the other, but another glittery pink nametag came into focus and she started to see stars in what remained of her vision. It said at the very top, Manager: Claire. Gertrude looked up into her face and oddly enough saw her winged eyeliner and red lips. The rest of her face came into a haphazard focus along with her long dark waves of hair that smelled faintly of plastic. Claire wrapped her arms gently around Gertrude's shoulders, her voice was kind, and reassuring. Even though Gertrude hadn't really heard what she had said. Claire turned them back around and headed toward the back of the store and through the private employee areas, Claire held her head high as she passed by the gawking customers and her staff. Gertrude clung to her with every ounce of dying strength she had. She lost all sense of time for a few minutes.

Gertrude was sitting in an overly plush chair with a hole in the arm when everything seemed to fade back to normal. Stuffing peaking out of the pink crushed velvet like clouds escaping. A cup of cheap but hot black coffee gripped in her hands as Sam was quietly reprimanded in the small office about touching clients without permission. It ended with Sam storming out and Claire looking relieved as she chucked Sams nametag into the trash bin. "You doing better there? Need me to call anyone?" Gertrude shook her head. Claire nodded and shut the door that led out to the storefront, ripping off the brown wig off her head and vibrant orange and red curls came out.

Gertrude smiled and pointed, "Suits you." Claire tousled her curls and nodded, "I know. But rules are rules and I have to cover up the most expensive thing in this place with a cheap wig. So you need a backless bra, what size do you know?" Gertrude felt the shakes creep back up, and Claire smiled at her reassuringly. "No judgment, and you're getting a free bra and if you are up to it dinner on me at our shitty food court." Gertrude nodded and stuffed it all back down inside, " 36 A."

***

Gertrude's eyes had lulled closed but she wasn't sleeping. Claire had slipped in quietly. She put her phone back in her oversized bag and sat down. It would have been hard to explain, the energy around her was a jumbled mess of mixed emotions. She had been like that for months. Her presence was a weight that Gertrude didn't know how to handle. She wanted to be there for her, but Claire was trying to be there for Gertrude. They didn't know where each other stood in this dance of sickness and health. Would she still want to be with her after all this? Would all of this change their dynamic?

Gertrude wasn't good at being mothered, she had little experience with genuine mothering, and Claire wanted to so very badly take care of her and help her through this. Gertrude couldn't linger on all these drug-induced feelings and emotions, Claire was shaking her awake from the fake sleep. Gertrude pushed all the doubt down in hopes they would get cut out soon enough.

"Babe, they are here to take you down." Claire's face was clear but her emotions were blurry and unclear. The room began trickling in with familiar and unfamiliar faces, who's emotions were also indistinguishable.

Finally. But then all Gertrude wanted was that damn burger.

Bare

Chapter 7

Sacrileges, Jokes & a Lesbian Wedding

It was so bright. Like stupidly bright in the room. And there was a bunch of blue surrounding her too. Not a pretty blue, but a muted steal blue, a dull murky sapphire. It was the blankets and scrubs; The blue gloves and blue cloths on metal trays. Blue scrub caps and blue shoe covers. A blindingly bright and nauseatingly Ceil blue sea of medicine at work. Even the sound was blue. That was when Gertrude realized she was very high.

Just as the sedative had begun to hit its peak, a team came in, and a tussle of excitement happened. Gertrude, who wasn't permitted to walk was removed from her machines and additional tubes place were placed in various places in her body, each equally as uncomfortable as the next, the last was painful despite the promise of a little pinch. Her blankets were shifted for fresh sterile ones. A hazy cap wrapped up her fuchsia and orange curls. They did a quick once over to ensure all of her piercings were removed, like she'd forget one, and she was given straight oxygen to breathe. Then finally her bed was laid back and loosed from the wall to move on it's hidden wheels.

Gertrude had been quiet as Claire and she said their "See you soon's." The numbness seeped all Gertrude's will out of her. Whether it was done purposefully or because of the meds she wasn't sure. Gertrude tried to fake it for Claire, but she knew it hadn't fooled anyone. Claire also failed to present a strong front and as the large metal doors scrapped open Gertrude heard her sob. Gertrude should care, she should have called out something, say "I love you." But she didn't. She couldn't.

The hallway passed by in a blur of cheap hotel art and somber faces that sucked at being reassuring. Gertrude took comfort in the fact that soon she would be in pitch black. Part of her hoped she wouldn't come back from all this. That it would end today.

The stress that had worn on all those she loved until they were smaller than they had been; it had chipped away too much from her. It had taken her hair. Her nightlife. Her sex life. Her job and sense of purpose. It had mangled the already dilapidated relationship with her mother and wore away the polish on her marriage. If had made her dog afraid for her and sometimes of her.

It had defemulated her and that wasn't even a real word. Gertrude's mind trailed over on the patriarchal bullshit that men had a strong word like emasculate and women had nothing. Her brain continued to trail over the way women had been treated historically and in her chemically induced haze and perseverated on all the ways this could go wrong due to the historical lack of study on the female body. Then her mind shifted quickly to something else and then she was lost again. Trying to recall the feeling so familiar and so distant.

Gertrude watched as if she had been outside her own body while the tubes were plugged into her port over and over again and poison pumped through her body. She watched as she vomited everything she had managed to eat that day all in one go, her body retching and writhing over the bucket since she couldn't make it to the bathroom. She watched as the radiation burned her skin and she fought not to cry out in pain as it liquified her insides. Gertrude watched as all the years of therapy to love her body and herself melt away as all that love coagulated inside her into betrayal and cancer.

It was all for naught. The cancer had spread

and the chemo hadn't done much. The doctors had offered more aggressive treatments and Claire was ready to jump on them, to keep fighting a war that was not waging in her body; but Gertrude said no, and now here they were.

Her arms were strapped down, out, and away from her body. Very reminiscent of when she saw the young men practicing for an Easter play at church and they took turns being the star of the show. It brought a small and likely morbid smile to Gertrude's face. "Bit sacrilegious don't you think?" Gertrude had asked the anesthesiologist, but he just blinked at her. All eyes, blue eyes, in a blue gown, cap, and mask. She chuckled for him as he stood and walked away.

The surgeon entered in a flurry and looked the situation over and then with a quick no-nonsense nod asked Gertrude, "You ready."

This was the moment, what she had been waiting for, and words failed her. She couldn't say anything. She just nodded, and then a smelly plastic cone slid over her face and the silent and judgmental anesthesiologist stared down at her.

* * *

Everyone stared at her. The music had dimmed, and the long table of friends sat there with big overly eager smiles on their faces. The waitresses were all frozen in time waiting for the cue. The smell of food went stagnant and all the guests turned to look in an equal blend of joy and disgust spread through the whole of the restaurant.

Gertrude had her hair tied up in a high bun, her black knee length dress suddenly felt far too hot and the beading felt far too itchy. Gertrude brought her attention to the very end of the table, a stern and unamused look bore into her soul. The daggers coming from them twisted her insides and deep seated shame rooted around in her gut. She wanted to vomit suddenly.

Gertrude thought they had moved past this, and found a rough tolerance of one another, but her mother was not one to sidestep her faith, even for her own children. Her mother with her gray curls and modest cream dress kept perfectly still, all save for her fingers as she squeezed the crucifix at her neck. Once again Gertrude was a scared little girl with her mother and her mother's preacher berating her and screaming scripture at her as she cried in a corner and wet herself. Gertrude remembered that day, her oldest brother Walter ran in and put himself between them. It landed him a black eye at home and he stopped defending her after that. It all that rushed back and then some. Gertrude felt herself shake under her mother's icy glare when smooth warm fingers squeezed hers, and she looked at Claire's beautiful and hopeful face. She looked up at Gertrude, the rose gold circle seeming suspended between them.

And then it was all gone. The smile overwhelmed Gertrude's face so much that it ached. She nodded without thinking, the wave of joy drowning out the prickles of the past in an instant. The gold band slid up her finger and almost simultaneously her arms slid around Claire. Their lips met and a smile and a kiss.

The restaurant erupted into a blend of overwhelming joy, with an aftertaste of disdain.

But it wasn't enough to take Gertrude back to the moment of terror. To the fear of her family and the judgment of others. The waitress surrounded them and the table with well wishes and a complimentary piece of cake.

Gertrude's other brother Oliver rushed and embraced her in his most welcome and trademark bear hugs. Lifting her off her feet with excitement. Gertrude laughed, keeping her eyes averted from the dark corner at the far end of the table. Oliver had left home a long time ago. He didn't understand why Gertrude stayed in touch with their family, to be honest, Gertrude didn't understand it either. Oliver put her down and another large hand gently squeezed her shoulder, and Sean was there with baby Max in his arms. Not really a baby anymore, she was more of a sass-talking toddler. Oliver and Sean had adopted her shortly after they got married, an event that only Gertrude and Claire went to. Walter and his wife Joy had been invited but everyone was sure that their mother had put her foot down.

"Congratulations little sis, we are so happy for you." Sean was full of pride and love as he spoke, the brother who claimed her, and she claimed him back. Oliver smiled mischievously and shouted, "Fuck yea! Lesbian Wedding! We just gatta find you a dress that makes it look like you got boobs girl!" Claire laughed and Gertrude tried, but the seething dark corner of the table was empty. She didn't even congratulate them.

✶ ✶ ✶

It was all very hazy. Like she was still in a dream she didn't remember having or even going to sleep. Gertrude didn't feel anything. Not just emotionally but physically. She was floating in a watercolor painting of numbness. That had to be a win.

There was a familiar whir of machines and lights around her, and the sound of far-away voices registered in her brain but they weren't visible to her yet. All she could see was a strange plastic tube coming up and out of her mouth, like an alien crawling out of her face and reaching out toward the foggy lights. She wanted to talk or reach out, but she couldn't.

Gertrude heard her then, like a knife through the butter of her mind, Claire was there. Her voice sounded calm and even a happy sob, or maybe it was a sorrowful laugh. The words came in and out.

"Everything went well-"
"All according to plan-"
"Resting comfortably-"
"-call her family-"

Gertrude tried to focus on them, tell them not to call anyone, her eyes tried to see what she couldn't, but the urge to fall back into the darkness claimed her. She just wanted to see Claire.

Chapter 8

Recovery Eviction & a Family Meeting

It hurt to breathe. Gertrude didn't want to open her eyes in case that made the pain worse. Which sounded stupid, but she didn't care. She just didn't want to hurt any worse than she did. Unfortunately, she had to shift her weight as her butt had the horrible pins and needles feeling that went down her legs. To safely do that she had to open her eyes.

The room was dim. Most of the lights were off and Claire was passed out sitting in the chair, she was tipped forward and her head resting on the foot of the bed. Her makeup was washed away and her skin looked so soft and dewy. Hair held back and away from her face with one of the black terry cloth headbands she liked to wear around the house on her self-care day it had an obnoxiously big bow on the front. Her soft snores were like a purring cat softly shaking the air by Gertrude's feet. Claire was beautiful, even in the hospital and all that was weighing on them, Gertrude's heart fluttered seeing her. And it wasn't the anesthesia.

Gertrude slowly moved her hands with great effort and placed them on either side of her. She took a deep steadying breath and then tried to to push her weight up and shift a bit to ease some of the discomfort in her rear. However, she wasn't prepared for her insides to tear apart under the tight bandages and the very visceral feeling that raged over her entire body. Suddenly her vision went white and Gertrude didn't hear it until it was too late, the scream of pain that had escaped her.

Claire shot up in a haze of alert but tired eyes as she stumbled to her feet. Drool and fear drained from her face as she shot up quickly, the chair clattering down on the hard tile floor behind her. Claire clasped the bed around Gertrude's head, careful not to touch her, Claire's panic-filled voice rolling out a series of near unintelligible questions. Gertrude squinted through the blinding agony to focus on Claires concern.

A machine must have gone off somewhere, or maybe they had heard her cry out, but Nurse Jodie came rushing in, and then very suddenly stopped short. Gertrude imagined the sight was alarming. With a loud and quick boom, she ordered Claire to leave the room. Gertrude felt the panic zap out of Claire and jump right into her. Gertrude tried to move her arms to grasp Claire's hands and hold her close, but couldn't move. She tried to will her hands to move again, but her body wouldn't. Two unknown nurses came in and with firm but kind hands, they guided Claire from the room. Gertrude was unable to say much and found she wasn't also couldn't reach her arms out to stop them. She felt the hot tears on her cheeks willing Claire with her mind to stay with her. But they evicted Claire from her room like she was a hindrance. Gertrude felt the hot tears that had seeped down her face hit her collarbones as she mumbled Claire's name.

Jodie, unfazed and borderline unfeeling, pressed the button on a small machine connected to the IV in Gertrude's arm. She tried to see around the looming form of Jodie and get a reassuring look from Claire, but she couldn't. Claire was gone. Gertrude didn't realize what was happening as a burning sensation ran up her arm and a metallic taste formed on her tongue, only then it was too late and the darkness began to claim her she realized, she really didn't like Nurse Jodie.

***

"She's just looking for attention again. Like every other big announcement in her life. She just wants us to pity her." Gertrude's mother sneered at her as she got up from the table. Her dad stayed stony and quiet, his overly passive nature like a shield his children had broken themselves against. Oliver was already exasperated at the situation and his silent pleas to his father went unreciprocated. Gertrude's oldest brother, Walter, and his wife Joy, had the decency to at least look shocked by what her mother had said and Joy even looked sympathetic for Gertrude. Claire sat at Gertrude's side, holding her up and being the pillar of strength that was needed especially today.

Oliver had never been the child to openly rebel he did it quietly. His court house elopement, and no social media attention adoption. He didn't bring his husband around for family events and bowed his head to pray at meal times. He left the room when politics was discussed and never mentioned who he voted for. He dressed in a manner his father could be proud of and displayed his Christian college diploma proudly in his home. He respected his mother and father, even if they couldn't respect him. He was the opposite of Gertrude, in every capacity. But today was the day he stopped trying to quietly garner their love and fought for the one he loved and who loved him.

"She is your fucking daughter and she told you she might die, that she's sick and scared and that's your response. To say she's looking for attention." Gertrude had never witnessed her cool as a cucumber brother so enraged he was shaking. The room maintained it's stunned silence as the heat came off her mother in damn near diabolical waves.

Her mother's eyes locked onto Oliver as her new target, and she leaned in closer to him, her voice thin and cold as ice. "She is just here to get her pity party. Half the world is sick with something, she doesn't need to draw attention to herself."

Joy stood then dragging Walter with her and gave Gertrude a small and sad smile. Joy gave Gertrude a small side hug. Her mother had died of breast cancer, so this couldn't have been easy. Shortly after her mom's passing, she met Walter at the church, and they had been together since. Gertrude liked her all in all. Joy gave Gertrude's dad a small pat on the shoulder and then left the room. She didn't speak to Gertrude's mother.

Walter gave Gertrude a nod and a small smile, a glimmer of the boy who protected her shimmering under the mirage of youth pastor and deacon of the church. Maybe it was meant to be reassuring, but for Gertrude, it was good to see that boy again. She missed him. He held out his hand to Claire and they had an awkward handshake before he followed his wife out the door. He said nothing to either of his parents.

Gertrude's mother turned back to her, "There are you happy girl? You force your brother and sister-in-law to leave."

Gertrude felt both Oliver and Claire tense with the impending retorts that had been building, but she stood before either of them could unleash it on her mother.

There was a lot she should say, but she neither had the courage or the will to say anything. She just turned and left. Oliver and Claire followed her, and as the walked down the old concrete steps she used to jump off as a child, her mother could be heard shouting, "You need to actually have breasts to get breast cancer."

Gertrude broke down when the got into Oliver's SUV.

✱ ✱ ✱

Consciousness came back slowly. But blissfully, pain-free. Gertrude reached out to where Claire's hand should have been. The bed next to her was cold and empty. Opening her eyes she saw her room was empty and she felt a small bit of panic. The curtains were closed, but the bright sun showed through the cracks in the fabric. She tried to piece together what had happened before, but it was all a bit too hazy. She remembered Jodie, but where was Claire?

A soft and well-timed knock echoed off the door and through the impersonal room. The warm and familiar face of Nurse Schultz popped in the door. She smiled widely and swept into the room with great gusto and form, her badge and keys jangling loudly at her hip. She carried with her a tray with brown little bowls that looked like they had been turned upside down on it. Her voice was calm and comforting, "You, my dear have been cleared to eat. So, as requested a burger and fries." Gertrude felt the smile pull at her lips and she raised a brow mockingly, "Is it a veggie burger, Sarah? And where's the chocolate shake?" Her voice was hoarse and throaty.

Aghast at the use of her first name, Nurse Schultz held back the tray but only for a moment, "It better be the meds making you talk to me that way. I'll take it back and put you on clear liquids for the rest of your stay." Gertrude laughed, the pain meds keeping her comfortable enough to do so when another knock came echoing through the room. Nurse Schultz's face went serious, and as she moved the tray closer she whispered, "Your wife is upset, but she wants to see you. Can I let her in?" Gertrude felt her face contort in confusion as she stuttered, "What-what happened?"

Nurse Schultz gave Gertrude's shoulder a reassuring squeeze, "A problem I dealt with. Nurse Jodie will not be on your case going forward." Still confused Gertrude nodded toward the door and Nurse Schultz shuffled over to open it. Claire filled the doorway with light, calm, and reassurance. All the doubt that Gertrude didn't know she had retreated into that locked dark place that Gertrude didn't need. Not today anyway.

CHAPTER 9

Manbun in Scrubs and a Bullshit Diagnosis

Gertrude felt the sweat dripping down her face as she shook, struggling to hold the weights a newborn baby could lift with ease. Her drainage tubes had finally been removed that morning after a slow and infection-filled healing process. It had led to many fever-fueled arguments, discussions, and laughing fits. Only about half of it Gertrude actually remembered. But it had been brought up numerous times.

Gertrude in her drug-induced haze had in fact accused nurse Jodie of wrongdoing, but cited the reason of, "Bigoted Bitch." Which wasn't a valid reason to throw her off the Medical Helipad, at least according to Oliver when he visited a few days after the surgery. Gertrude had suggested other things, like getting strippers and buying Portugal. Also, buying Portugal for the strippers. It had been a hectic and delusional few weeks.

But earlier this week the fever had broken, her blood counts started to get normal and the third round of antibiotics had finally done the trick. She had hoped they would just give her a few days to rest before making her do anything really physical, but nothing had happened how it should. Now she was weaker than a newborn kitten and the medical team started her on Physical Therapy early in the hopes it would help her regain her strength.

Gertrude's arms painfully collapsed down to

her sides and the therapist gave her a kind and reassuring smile. He was cute in his baby blue scrub pants and the patterned scrub shirt with sweatbands and little hand weights in a bunch of colors all over it. He had a man bun, which would have been a disappointment normally, but with his sharp bone structure, he made it look good. A bit too good. He had even managed to turn Claire's head, and she had no attraction to men, or so she said. Oliver practically drooled until his husband, Sean, handed him a paper towel.

Everything had started to develop a kind of inorganic normalcy despite the abnormal circumstances Gertrude had resided in, and even that would change here in a few days. The therapist packed up his little blue push cart and patted Gertrude's knee gently. "Tomorrow you will do better, just rest now." He headed for the door and turned giving her a thumbs up and a wink, "Great job Gertie!" Suddenly he became very unattractive. But only for a second. The door shut behind him and Gertrude looked up at the board, the doctor on call's name mocked her with the start of this shit show. She didn't want to see him, so she reached slowly for her phone to video chat Claire and her dog Albert.

* * *

The doctor had looked startled, but some deep-seated decorum in him was a glutton for punishment as he asked Claire, "I am sorry what was that?" Claire unfazed and unperturbed stared him dead in the face. "It's bullshit, test again." Gertrude however said nothing.

She hadn't known per se, it wasn't like a gut feeling or some instinct that nagged at her. She had gone through the motions just like every poster in every OBGYN office she had ever been to, advised her to do. But neither had she been hopeful. She had been numb about it, and this time unintentionally. She didn't open that locked darkness and let it consume her, this came on naturally with blood work, ultrasounds, mammograms, and then biopsies.

It had crept in one spiny black coil at a time wrapping around her intimacy, strangling her compassion, and draining the joy from her smile.

She felt the coldness and the cynicism disintegrate the warm edges of some of her friendships and even caused friction between her and Oliver.

The past month had been trying for her and Claire too. Gertrude's carefree attitude toward this whole thing had caused tension and while Claire had been eager to cancel clients and shift bookings and make Gertrude's appointments. Gertrude just wanted to go get coffee and read her book. She didn't have the strength or desire to shuffle from doctor to doctor; appointment to appointment.

It wasn't until this moment, right there, with one word Gertrude understood that she had given up. She didn't have the stomach to fight. Or maybe she didn't have the heart. It felt like divine irony that as her life had finally come together, Gertrude finds out all of this crap, and for it all to fall apart again. She was back to the starting point, alone and nothing but an inconvenience.

The doctor pushed his too thin glasses for his too pudgy face and said flatly, "Ma'am I need you to calm down or you will wait outside for the rest of your sisters' appointment. I will finish this conversation in a civilized manner." That drew Gertrude out of her mist, and she simply said, "Wife. She's my wife."

The doctor's brow furrowed as he looked down and flipped through the papers, color easing up his cheeks making him look like a cooking pig, only he smelled far worse, and he nodded in a feigned apology, "My mistake. Wife"

Gertrude nodded and put her hand in Claire's and pushed a monotone smile up on her face asking the doctor, "So what is next? Hospice?" Claire gasped and squeezed Gertrude's hand so tight the knuckles cracked. The doctor shook his head the smile an uneven shape and torn between being uncomfortable and amused. "Nothing that extreme, we aren't there yet. We aren't even close to there. But I will recommend counseling. A good therapist is going to be-" Gertrude interrupted him, "I have a therapist." He bit off the rest of what he was saying.

Claire unable to let it drop, slammed her hand on his desk, shouting. All the anger Gertrude should have felt, poured out of Claire, "No. This is not right, Check again."

His face grew dark, and with a sad sigh, he just said, "I am sorry, but it is breast cancer. We are certain."

Gertrude laughed then, she didn't know why, and she hadn't meant to. But she laughed out loud agreeing suddenly with Claire. "It is bullshit." The doctor looked concerned as Gertrude continued, laughing so hard she was crying, "I don't even have boobs."

*\ *\ *

Gertrude had managed to lift the tiny weights slowly over her head and then lower them down again. Two reps were all she had managed, and if anyone had seen her physical therapist celebrating, they would have thought she ran first place in a triathlon. His celebration was big and infectious. Gertrude couldn't help but laugh. He helped her ease her arms back down to her sides and he grabbed her stylish hospital cup full of water and helped her take a sip. She tried not to take too deep of breaths, she didn't want to pop a stitch, but she was tired. Happy, but tired.

"Alright Gertrude, let's get you standing, and let's try doing that out to the side and back to center." Gertrude felt the exasperated smile light up her face and she nodded and kicked her legs off the side of the bed. She slowly reached out to him for balance, "Alright, help me up."

She did four reps.

CHAPTER 10

Promise of Sushi & a Rained out Dates

Gertrude was very annoyed they wouldn't just let her just walk out of the hospital. But no she had to get pushed in a wheelchair like some timid old lady with moldy sweets in her pockets and a memory that failed two decades prior. Claire had even joked about getting a seatbelt for her if Gertrude tried to get up, she had not been amused. She just wanted to be independent for the first time in a month and do something for herself. Even something as minor as walking out a door.

However, that didn't seem likely to happen so long as Claire had a discharge list ten miles long and three weeks of clear calendar to baby Gertrude. She knew she'd be lucky if she got to pee on her own while Claire was on this sabbatical with her.

Oliver had thankfully agreed to meet them at the condo, he was bringing a "Butt ton of sushi" and promised to feed Gertrude like he used to when she was a toddler in her highchair and she poured spaghetti all over his head. Gertrude had no recollection of this event, but it was one of the few happy memories that could be brought up with the family that didn't have some underlying pain, for her or them. She was looking forward to the sushi, less to him trying to feed her.

Nurse Schultz trailed behind them, she chatted cordially with Claire. She was a sight to behold, carrying a nerdy blanket and a large stuffed dino. All while towing a big glittery suitcase behind her. The large glass entry doors were pushed open as a kind-looking security guard tipped his hat to Gertrude and then shared a quick hushed conversation with Nurse Schultz.

Everyone seemed to have the sun under their skin and the wind in their hair. The happiness and joy flowed off them in waves. Gertrude tried to take it in and enjoy it. Compared to the darkness she had inhabited for months it was both a welcome and terrifying experience. The number of muddled emotions had piled up around her and she had almost been drowning in them. Gertrude was hoping to sort them all out and knew her first act as a free woman was to get a therapist appointment. After she mourned what she needed to and celebrated what she could, and maybe figure out how to actually define the difference between the two.

They stepped out into the warm early summer air, filled with pollen and the smell of pizza from across the street. The parking lot was bustling with the outpatient visits and visitors of the day.

Everyone was going in and Gertrude had finally escaped the confines of the hospital. Eager to stand and get out of the sympathy mobile, she tried kicking the footrests of her wheelchair up when a warmer hand gently patted her shoulder.

Joy, her sister-in-law, smiled down at her. Her golden cross necklace glinted in the sun. An unexpected site that left Gertrude literally speechless. Claire made a happy comment to her that Gertrude missed entirely and then wheeled up to a van Gertrude wasn't familiar with. Joy and Claire packed Gertrude's stuff into the back. Before she climbed in, Gertrude turned to Nurse Schultz. She gave her a light, but emotional hug before being helped into the back seat. The door slid shut, and the van moved gently forward.

Joy looked back at her from the rearview mirror, all genuine smiles, and said, "Ready to go home?" Gertrude nodded and turned her face up to the bright and warm sun.

***

Gertrude stared out the window in spite, the twilight closing in on them in that weird way where the ground was much darker than the violet and blush sky above them. The clouds had slowly rolled in and while raining you could still see the stars and fading daylight through the black clouds. Rain trailed the glass in curvy streaks that Gertrude couldn't help but envy. Ripples moved in no particular rhythm as the glass began to fog with the breath of so much said, and even more left unsaid. The air was warm, despite the chill from the sudden weather shift.

Gertrude wouldn't look at Claire, instead, she fiddled with her wedding band and tugged at wayward loose strings of her ripped jeans. Anything that kept her attention anywhere but the very angry woman in the driver's seat. Claire repeated herself one more time really striving to drive the point to a home it didn't have, "You are strong enough to do this. It's not major surgery, it's just more aggressive chemo. If it doesn't work we can talk about more drastic options, but I want you to try first. Please, babe." Gertrude answered in a complete and full sentence. Two letters, one word, a full sentence. "No."

Claire threw up her hands in frustration. Her sobbing blended with anger that made her whole body shake as she spoke, "Why won't you fight this? Why won't you fight for your body? You're so fucking beautiful and smart, and somehow so stupid too." Gertrude knew Claire didn't mean it. She lashed out harshly when she was angry. She had been going to therapy for that, but when Gertrude got her diagnosis, Claire put so much on the back burner. She had stopped taking care of herself and focused on Gertrude, which she felt guilty about. Claire slammed her fists suddenly into the steering wheel, a small belt of the horn rung out and died quickly as the rain started to fall harder. Grey sheets washed away the outside and left them alone and abandoned.

Gertrude felt small then, she knew she looked small, and she sounded small when she managed the words, "I don't want to fight my own body, Claire." That made Claire stop. Her face was streaked with the eyeliner and mascara she had meticulously applied for this date. The lip stain still hung on strong, but loose bits of turquoise curls had escaped their bobby pin. She looked perfect, even with the streaks of charcoal and navy ran down her beautiful cheeks. Even when she wiped it all away, Gertrude's breath would still catch seeing Claire. And now she was so raw and scared there next to Gertrude. Claire hadn't intended on all these tears or an argument so she hadn't used the waterproof stuff, but maybe the streaks of eyeliner would pave the way to a painful understanding.

Gertrude's insides were twisted, not just literally with the cancer, but metaphorically. If she had been honest with herself maybe it wasn't just the idea of fighting her own body, maybe it had been the idea of fighting for her womanhood.

Gertrude remembered seeing how her mother defined being a woman, and suddenly Gertrude's life had veered off course and she was a creature to be managed and trained. Her body was suddenly too shapely and then in a few short years not shapely enough. She looked like a little boy and was told to dress more feminine. She looked like a harlot and was told to dress more conservatively. Her boobs were too small. Her attractions went the wrong way. Her womanhood as defined by her past, was nonexistent. Gertrude wanted to define it for herself going forward.

A tight and painful knot formed in Gertrude's throat as she tried to keep her composure, "Will I not be enough for you if I do this? Will you leave me?"

The air crackled with thunder and painful silence as the storm continued to roll in around their little hybrid car. Sheets of water danced in lines across the windshield.

Claire opened her mouth to speak, but Gertrude cut her off, talking too fast, "All my life has been a war with my body until I found you. You helped me love myself. Little boobs and all. You helped me see me, and then let me shine all on my own. I know this is hard for you and not the choice you would make, but this is my choice. And if you can't love me after all this, then you were not who I fell in love with. I want to make my choices, I want to be the woman I want to be, whether I have tits or not. I want to define me. Not my mother, not society, and not you-" Gertrude stumbled with that, it was painful to say,

"But me. Let me choose how I want to live and live with me."

If it had been silent, it would have been deafening. Gertrude was thankful for the torrents of water beating against the windows. Claire had silent tears rolling down her face and she sniffled loudly and ungracefully. She took a deep but shaky breath and clasped Gertrude's hand. Gertrude stared down at her own dark glittery nails, a stark contrast to the bright blue and green swirled on Claire's nails as their fingers intermingled.

Gertrude was not sure where the conversation would end. Claire squeezed gently and Gertrude was slow to meet her gaze, but all Claire said was, "Ok. Your call." Gertrude felt like all the air left the car and felt her chest heave with a large intake of much needed air, "OK?" Claire nodded, "Ok."

Claire wiped her hands across her face and smeared her makeup even more, giggled and made the most ridiculous and entertaining request. 'Let's throw a bye-bye boobies party!"

Gertrude felt lighter, easier. The world shifted from the strange and uncomfortable thing she had been wading through for months, into the warm and familiar. She nodded happily, a party sounded great.

*** * * ***

Joy and Claire shouted angrily at her as she unbuckled her seatbelt and gracelessly climbed out of the van and practically penguin walked to the hunter green door of their condo. The rose bushes were starting to bud, and Claire had hung up the wind chimes. Their chairs had the black summertime pillows on them that said, "Wine and Sun" and the matching outdoor rug was rolled out. The Skeleton gnomes watering her small little garden had been put out and it was the most welcome sight. Gertrude couldn't have the wine mentioned on her pillows yet, but soon enough.

She braved the steps and made it to the second before the throbbing around her ribcage became too intense she had to slowly lower herself down onto the brick steps to slow her breathing. The bandages while not tight, still made her feel like she was wearing some kind of corset. She was sure nothing was loose or bleeding but it still hurt like it was.

Claire and Joy walked up, concern mingled with annoyance played across both their faces when the door behind Gertrude opened and a playfully heated discussion between Walter and Oliver poured out along with a snorting and snuffling Albert who missed Gertrude so much. Gertrude tried to turn to look at them, but the pain was too much and she settled with a stiff and awkward lean. Walter scooped up Albert as best as he could given that Albert was obese for a bulldog and his weight clocked in at 65 pounds. It was more of a grab and hold on for dear life and less of a scoop.

Oliver shook his head, annoyed but not surprised to find her down on the porch. It took another fifteen minutes to get Gertrude inside and settled into the corner of the couch, Albert curled up next to her his quiet woofs told her that's where he planned to stay. The table had a modest but delicious-looking sushi spread on it, every color of the rainbow all splayed out for the munching. Claire came over and sat next to her, her fingers finding Gertrude's and intertwining.

Tomorrow she had a follow-up appointment and more physical therapy. Tonight she had pain meds, sushi, her dog, and her family.

CHAPTER 11

Shoe Shopping and Bare Chested

In the year and a half since her surgery, Gertrude hadn't really gone shopping for clothes, of any kind. Now she was in a lingerie store and she held up a skimpy, strappy number with purple rosettes flowering off the garment at very opportune locations. It was so feather light that calling it breathable would have been an understatement. But that's what the tag said, breathable. Gertrude put it down and turned to Oliver with a shrug. "I don't know if it's me." He loudly rolled his eyes and picked up a stretchy green number with a babydoll top, "Well it's not really about you, it's about Claire. What about this, green is her favorite."

Gertrude laughed, "Green was her favorite. And it is about me too, I have to be comfortable wearing it." Oliver side-eyed her and shook his head, "Sis, you just have to look good stripping it off. Your comfort isn't important for ten seconds" Gertrude softly punched him in the shoulder and pulled out another purple ensemble. Realizing there were far too many buckles for it to be worth her while she put it back, purposefully forgetting to address his last comment as she continued, "Purple is her go too now. She wants to redo the entire bedroom in it. She even bought these horrible sheets."

Oliver had the decency to look annoyed for her, "Again?" Gertrude shrugged and moved to a different rack of clothing, this one all leather and feathers. Gertrude took one inquisitive look and then decided that would be something best to be picked out with Claire present.

She sidestepped over to the section marked clearance, hoping Oliver wouldn't notice her trying to do frugal but sexy simultaneously, and flipped through the mediocre choices. In his world, frugal and sexy don't co-exist. She continued to flick through the hangers, nothing truly catching her eye, or nothing in her size. Gertrude was about to give up when she heard a bit of a ruckus on the other side of the store. She popped her head out from behind a gilded bustier designed for someone with breasts the size of her torso to see Oliver tugging a box out of a lady's hands. His face contorted in determination as it slipped out of her fingers and he turned and ran in Gertrude's direction. A hanger with an unidentifiable plum garment flapping comedically behind him the box clutched to his chest.

The angry customer shouted in Oliver's wake, "They aren't even your size!" To which Oliver shouted back over his shoulder, "And your wide feet would have looked horrible in them and you need to shave your big toe lady!" The lady went red and stormed away in a furry.

Gertrude dashed behind a shelf with various binders and padding on them, hoping to hide from whatever mayhem Oliver had brought down on them, only to be unsuccessful as he slid on next to her. His smile wide and all teeth as he announced, "Bitch, I got the perfect outfit! Including shoes." His loud panting sent Gertrude into fits of laughter. This was going to be a fun opening night.

***

Gertrude picked at the peeling polish on her nails. The regret settled in like indigestion and Gertrude wished she had asked Claire to go with her to the appointment. Gertrude was pushing everyone for some normalcy and Claire doing other people's makeup was normal. So Gertrude encouraged her to go and be the head MUA for this semi-professional musical that had come into town. It had offered Claire to be head of the department and even to assist design some of the costumes. It was an amazing opportunity and Gertrude had pushed Claire into taking it. Oliver and Sean had finally put paperwork in to adopt a sibling for Max, now that she was almost in elementary school they had more time on their hands and Gertrude was not a fan of that being directed at her.

Walter and Joy actually found themselves in a series of doctor's appointments, and Gertrude was excited to find out she would be an Aunt on both fronts. She knew Joy was going to be a great mom, but the morning sickness hadn't worn off into the second trimester, so Gertrude tried not to bug her, just bring her ginger ale and lime sherbet, which is all she seemed to crave.

Gertrude really wanted to have someone there at that moment, but she didn't want to be a hindrance again and everyone was busy. They were months away from opening night, or either of the new arrivals but Gertrude still couldn't shake that feeling that she truly was an "Attention seeking leech that drained the life out of everything and everyone around her." Or whatever her mother had called her over and over again while she was alive.

She pushed the thoughts from her mind. The should'a, could'a, wouldas didn't help and Gertrude decided it would be best if she focused on where she was. Her arms were a little sore from the mere three gallons they had drained from her to do blood tests. They had given her a list but she summed it up that they would test her for everything that one person could be tested for. She was incredibly hungry from the fasting they had made her do and planned on eating a whole mushroom and feta pizza when she was out of here.

She had been poked and prodded. She had been covered with goo and had machines on sticks rubbed all over her, and then she was shoved into a loud tube and forced to listen to really bad country music. She just wanted to get home and curl up in her bed with her dog and sleep the rest of this nightmare away. But here she was sitting in this room again, this time alone, and she needed answers.

The office hadn't changed much since the last

time she had been in here, and as the doctor came in and sat down, he seemed to visibly note the vacant seat next to Gertrude and had the audacity to look relieved. Sure, Claire had screamed at him and called him bullshit the last time they were here, but this time would be different. It had better fucking be different. Gertrude felt everything go tense in her body, even her stomach stopped complaining.

The Doctor flipped through a series of pages in Gertrude's folder and then typed a bit in the computer and pulled up her imaging. He turned his screen for her to see. Gertrude didn't know what she was looking at, but leaned in to look anyways, trying to impress on him that she knew exactly what she was looking at, or at least had some idea.

The hazy images plastered on his screen all had her name stamped on them, along with numbers and measurements she didn't understand. They looked like black and white blobs with no discernible pattern. The next image was her chest x-ray, at least she knew what that was.

The doctor tutted loudly and removed his glasses, placing them silently on the desk. His face was unreadable and he rubbed his eyes. Gertrude physically braced herself, fire ants eating at her stomach. "All clear."

Gertrude sucked in her breath in shock and relief. Everything since going home had been going well, too well. Gertrude was convinced the cancer was back or that something was going to go wrong.

The doctor smiled. Genuine and heartfelt. He patted her hand, like something a grandfather might do. "Well we will still see you back in six months to stay on top of everything, but I am feeling good about it. Good enough to talk about augmentation."

That caught Gertrude off guard. She knew it had been a possibility and that a lot of women chose to do it, but she never thought about it for herself. She had just learned to truly love her body when it decided it hated her and mutated into cancer. And she was working twice a week to get there again with her therapist. Would implants help? Would Claire want her to have them? Would she want to go through healing all over again?

The doctor proceeded to tell her about her options, and that if she wanted to be more, and he stumbled over these words, well endowed compared to what she was, it was something they could work up to. Not just implants, but bigger boobs?

Gertrude had no answer. She looked down, easy enough to see her skinny legs and skull-embroidered jeans when there wasn't anything there to obstruct the view, and there hadn't been much originally. The doctor must have sensed something roiling around Gertrude and as reassuring and kindly as he could, he told her, "You could claim for feminity back, you could be a whole woman again."

He had meant well, despite the stab it was to Gertrude.

* * *

Gertrude took out the long black and green earrings she had been wearing for the show and tucked them into the little box on the sink vanity. Her short curls pinned back away from her face were itching to break free of their clips. Her hair was coming in faster now and this pixie cut look she had going on suited her, with a bit of vivid color she might even love it. She made a mental note to make a hair appointment. Gertrude loosed the clips and tousled her soft curls and they sprang back to life in wild and carefree directions.

Claire was humming loudly in the bedroom, the wine definitely giving her a happy buzz and she could be heard stumbling about, but that's what two and a half bottles did to Claire. Opening night was a big success. The show was a hit and her work with the actors looked amazing. Gertrude was so proud of Claire. Everyone was proud of her, Oliver, Sean, and Max. Even Walter and Joy came to see, managing to get a babysitter for Gertrude's new niece and goddaughter Charli. That was a fun event, Her and Claire were named Godmothers, and Oliver and Sean were named godfathers.

The Minister didn't know what to make of it, but Walter stood firm and reminded him that god told them to love all. The minister had no retort and did the ceremony. Gertrude had invited her dad, to both the baptism and Claire's show, but her calls to him went unreturned, and Gertrude chose not to be sad about it.

Gertrude pulled off the thin and slinky green dress she had been wearing that night. It hugged the curves she had and suited her frame wonderfully, with a sassy slit that went up to her thigh. She felt confident in the dress with its low back and cowl neckline. It was a first for her since her surgery.

Gertrude took a long look in the big mirror in the bathroom. Her long beaded necklace fell down her sternum and between where her breasts had been. She turned to the side, acutely looking over the flatness of her chest, and admired the hard-earned scars she had there. The lines where doctors fought cancer, and Gertrude fought the doctors. The marks where life and death could have intermingled. They were healed over, soft lined and relatively smooth scar tissue. She looked no smaller than she had before, and it was still her in that reflection. Still Gertrude. Still a woman.

Gertrude turned back to look head-on, the lacy number that had matched Oliver's 'Perfect shoes', rested on the vanity next to her. A cute little babydoll style nighty, with an empire waist and pearly black buttons. It was gauzy and looked like smoke in the air. Gertrude had worn the other undergarments with the dress and still had the shoes on her feet. They fit like a dream. Who didn't love a cute T-Strap Peep toe? Gertrude shuddered at that thought, she sounded a bit too much like Oliver.

Sliding the nighty over her shoulders smoothly she took one last look and smiled. She was pretty. Gertrude opened the door and Claire who was clumsily trying to remove her own shoes stopped dead and stared in awe. It wasn't the wine that had her freeze up and stumble to form a sentence.

"Fuck it" Gertrude ripped off the babydoll top and went bare.

The End

Bare

Acknowledgment

I don't know where to even begin. Thank you to my family, for their unending support, meals delivered to my desk, and constant motivation even when I was clocking in 40+ hours a week at the "real job". To my Mother-in-law for tolerating long hours and helping her son, my husband, accomplish the impossible. To my mom for the video chats to distract the kids.

To my husband, who on more than 10,000 occasions stepped up as both parents when I had the urge to write or edit or brainstorm.

A special thank you to T.M.Knoll for understanding I had to walk away from something to make this happen. I hope you can forgive me and all my failures. To V.Knoll, I miss you all the time farmer boy; Be proud of your Mom she has kicked butt, even mine a few times.

There are too many more to thank in this small space, I could write another hundred pages of thanks. Aunt Mary, my sister in law, my niece Doodle, Derrald, Claire, my monster kids. Seriously I can't fit it all on one page, but you know you are.

Thank you all. To my amazing Beta readers:

- *Julia Adams*
- *Alice Parker*
- *Erin Rogers Alderson*
- *Barbie Carr*
- *Sarah Schultz*
- *Amanda Harris*

I can't thank you all enough for the absolutely critical role you played, especially in the final leg of this, and for giving me advice as I ventured into a genre I don't typically read, let alone write.

To Barbie, the most patient long distance Model and friend I could have ever asked for. Thank you for being vulnerable and doing that stellar shot. I wasn't sure at all about the cover until you sent me that. It all made sense after that! Thank you and I miss you so much!

To fellow self-published author, beta reader, and the best cheerleader ever Amanda Harris. I know I drive you nuts with my unending questions, my self-doubt, and my constant bugging. But thank you, for everything, words will never be enough for the support you have shown me. If anyone actually reads this, go show her some love, and support her author journey, she deserves it way more than I do. Her books are also on Amazon!

For every person who has ever waged war on their body, regardless of the kind of battle. You are beautiful. You are worthy. You are valid. And your journey is important. Keep going.

For my stubborn grandmother, who believed in me from the very day I entered this world, to the moment she left it. I love you so much, and I never said it enough, and didn't show it enough, but I try to honor you now, every day. But, I did it, I wrote a book. I wish you were here to see it, to read it, and to celebrate it with me. I miss you Nina. - TC

Bare

ABOUT THE AUTHOR

Letti Raye Greene is a long-time and avid reader, Jane Eyre Collector, mom of three wild monsters, and a feral wife to an Air Force Veteran. Born in North Carolina, she lived the majority of her life in Michigan and now lives in Upstate New York with her crazy but loving and supportive in-laws. Fueled by Sushi and Coffee; she obviously enjoys reading, binging historical dramas, going on adventures with her family, dismantling the patriarchy, collecting Nerdy memorabilia, getting tattoos with her bestie, and buying Gnome decor for her home.

She is a Full-time Insurance Underwriter and advocate for her autistic son.

You can connect with me on:
https://lettirayegreeneauthor.com
https://www.facebook.com/BookWyrmWriting
TikTok: @b00kwyrmm
Instagram: Book_Wyrm_Writing

Author Photo taken by Melinda Parker-Fish in Glens Falls, NY

Bare

Coming Soon by Letti Raye Greene:

Book One of

The Lacuna Trilogy

Bare

Letti Raye Greene

Made in the USA
Middletown, DE
11 February 2025

71111683R00080